SUPER POTATO

#3 SUPER POTATO'S MEGA TIME-TRAVEL ADVENTURE

ARTUR LAPERLA

Graphic Universe™ • Minneapolis

Story and illustrations by Artur Laperla
Translation by Norwyn MacTíre

First American edition published in 2019 by Graphic Universe™

Graphic Universe™
A division of Lerner Publishing Group, Inc.
241 First Avenue North
Minneapolis, MN 55401 USA

For reading levels and more information, look up this title at www.lernerbooks.com.

Main body text set in CCWildWords 8.5/10. Typeface provided by Comicraft.

Library of Congress Cataloging-in-Publication Data

Names: Laperla (Artist) author, illustrator.
Title: Super Potato's mega time-travel adventure / Artur Laperla ; translation by Norwyn MacTíre.
Other titles: Super Patata. 3. English | Mega time-travel adventure
Description: First American edition. | Minneapolis : Graphic Universe, 2019. | Series: Super Potato ; book 3 | Originally published in Spanish: Barcelona : Bang Ediciones, 2014. | Summary: "Super Potato travels back in time in an effort to prevent his transformation from man into potato" —Provided by publisher.
Identifiers: LCCN 2018036038 (print) | LCCN 2018042006 (ebook) | ISBN 9781541561144 (eb pdf) | ISBN 9781512440232 (lb : alk. paper)
Subjects: LCSH: Graphic novels. | CYAC: Graphic novels. | Superheroes—Fiction. | Time travel—Fiction. | Potatoes—Fiction. | Humorous stories.
Classification: LCC PZ7.7.L367 (ebook) | LCC PZ7.7.L367 Sw 2019 (print) | DDC 741.5/973—dc23

LC record available at https://lccn.loc.gov/2018036038

Manufactured in the United States of America
1-42292-26142-10/22/2018

ONE FINE AFTERNOON WITH PROFESSOR ROSE . . .
CORTEX
Center for Advanced Research
THANK YOU FOR COMING, MR. POTATO.
SUPER POTATO, IF YOU DON'T MIND.

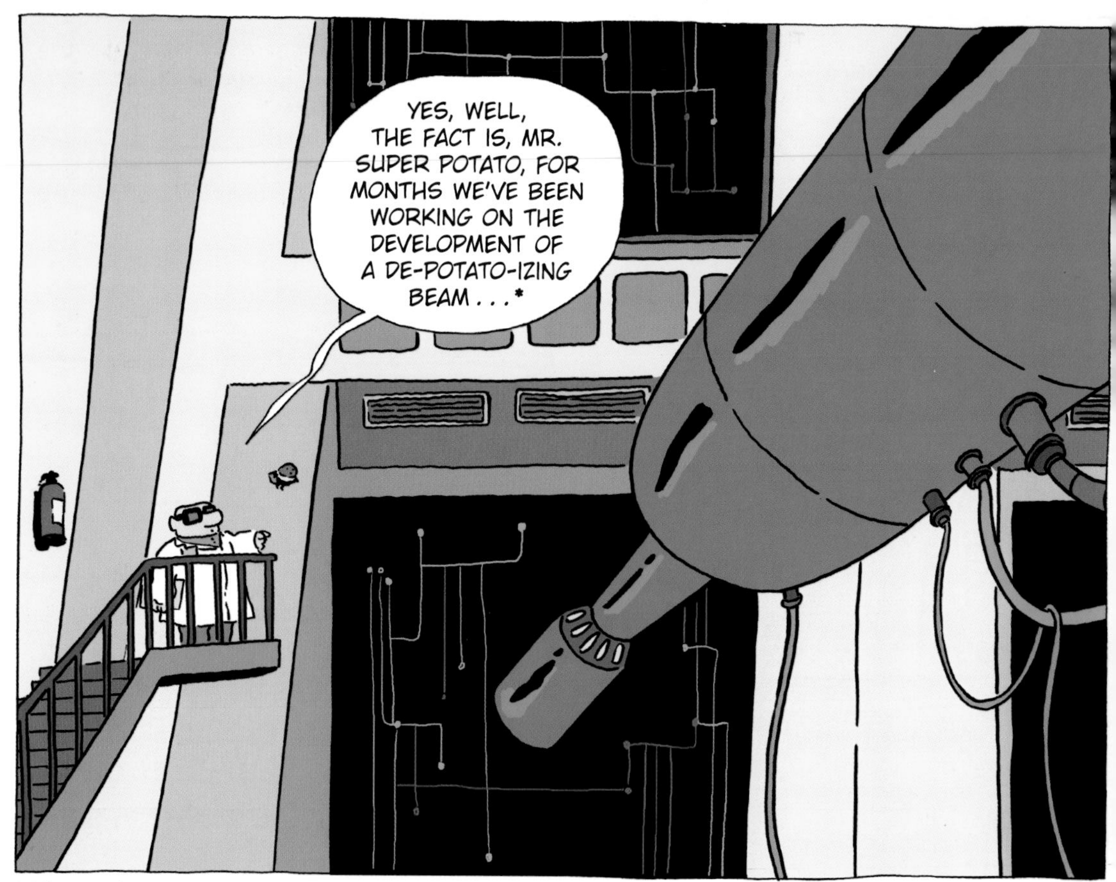

*IT'S TRUE! AS EVERYONE KNOWS (AND IF YOU DON'T, JUST READ THE FIRST BOOK IN THIS SERIES), SUPER POTATO IS REALLY SUPER MAX, TURNED INTO A TUBER BY THE POTATO-IZING BEAM OF THE EVIL DOCTOR MALEVOLENT.

UNFORTUNATELY, WE DON'T KNOW HOW TO MAKE IT WORK.
AT THE MOMENT, IT ONLY HELPS DEFROST FROZEN PIZZAS.
BUT DON'T DESPAIR.
WE'VE INVENTED A SIMPLER GADGET THAT MAY STILL BE OF INTEREST TO YOU.
THE ***SMALL-TIME MACHINE!***

THANKS TO THE SMALL-TIME MACHINE, YOU CAN TRAVEL BACK TO THE RECENT PAST AND DEFEAT DOCTOR MALEVOLENT BEFORE HE EVER USES THE POTATO-IZING BEAM AGAINST YOU!
IT'S REALLY SOMETHING, HUH?

WELL? WHAT DO YOU THINK? YOU HAVE THE FINAL SAY, MR. SUPER POTATO.
YES . . . I . . . THE TRUTH IS . . .
THE TRUTH IS THAT OUR HERO HAS GROWN ACCUSTOMED TO BEING SUPER POTATO. HE EVEN THREW OUT ALL THE EXPENSIVE SHAMPOOS AND CONDITIONERS HE USED WHEN HE WAS SUPER MAX.
BUT IT'S ALSO TRUE THAT A LITTLE PIECE OF SUPER MAX STILL LIVES INSIDE SUPER POTATO.
WHAT ARE YOU WAITING FOR, BUD? IT'S OUR CHANCE TO BE A TALL, HANDSOME HUMAN AGAIN!
UMM . . .
YEAH! OKAY!
I'LL GO BACK IN TIME!

WE EXPECTED NOTHING LESS!
WE'LL NEED A FEW HOURS TO PROGRAM THE MACHINE CORRECTLY.
CAN YOU COME BACK TOMORROW MORNING?
AND PLEASE AVOID ANY HEAVY MEALS.

SUPER POTATO RETURNS HOME . . .
TOMORROW . . .
. . . FEELING MORE THAN A LITTLE NERVOUS.

FOR DINNER, HE ONLY ALLOWS HIMSELF TO HAVE THREE COOKIES, A GLASS OF MILK, AND A SIGH.
CRUNCH, CRUNCH
SIGH.

THAT NIGHT HIS SLEEP IS FULL OF NIGHTMARES.
I... I...
ROSE-COLORED NIGHTMARES, BUT NIGHTMARES.
I'M YOU, AND YOU'RE ME!
YOU'RE WRONG!
I'M **DOCTOR MALEVOLENT!**
AND YOU'RE **NOBODY!**
AAH!
AAAH!
FORTUNATELY, EVEN THE LONGEST NIGHT GIVES WAY TO A NEW DAY.

CORTEX
Center for Advanced Research
WE'RE ALL SET!
JUST ENTER THE SMALL-TIME MACHINE'S PORTAL, AND YOU'LL APPEAR IN SUPER MAX'S HOUSE ONE HOUR BEFORE DOCTOR MALEVOLENT HITS HIM WITH THE POTATO-IZING BEAM.
REMEMBER—THE PORTAL WILL CLOSE BEHIND YOU.

THE PORTAL WILL OPEN AGAIN, THREE HOURS LATER, IN THE SAME PLACE.
WE DON'T KNOW HOW LONG WE CAN KEEP IT OPEN, SO DON'T DAWDLE. UNDERSTAND?
DEFINITELY. LET'S DO THIS!
HOW BRAVE! WHAT A ROLE MODEL.
SCIENCE WILL OWE YOU A DEBT.
AND YOU'LL OWE A BIT TO SCIENCE TOO.
ALL RIGHT, ALL RIGHT . . . HERE I GO!

SUPER POTATO HURLS HIMSELF TOWARD THE PORTAL . . .
. . . AND DISAPPEARS INTO THE TIME STREAM!
SO DIZZY . . .

IT'S IMPOSSIBLE TO TRAVEL THROUGH SPACE AND TIME WITHOUT SOME SLIGHT DISCOMFORT . . .
AAAAAAAH!!

. . . BUT HOW LONG CAN THIS LAST?
UGHHHH!
THANKFULLY, THE WORST IS OVER SOON.
NEXT STOP . . .
AAAHH . . .

THE PAST! THE WAY THINGS USED TO BE . . .
MIRROR, MIRROR, ON THE WALL, WHO'S THE HANDSOMEST SUPERHERO OF THEM ALL?

HUH!?
AAHHH . . .
PLOP
WHAT A DISGUSTING BUG!
UGHHHHH!
WHO SENT YOU?
PRINCESS SKELETON? ZOLTAN THE DARK?
SUPER MAX HAS A LONG ENEMIES LIST.
WHEW.

ATTENTION, SUPER MAX! CAN YOU HEAR ME?
GENERAL! WHAT'S GOING ON?
IT'S DOCTOR MALEVOLENT! HE'S STOLEN A PRICELESS STATUE FROM THE CITY MUSEUM!
DOCTOR MALEVOLENT!
YOU!
DON'T YOU MOVE.
I HAVE TO GO OUT, BUT . . .
UHHH . . .

. . . I'LL RETURN!
WAIT!
POOR SUPER POTATO! HE'S TOO WEAK TO FOLLOW SUPER MAX.
I . . . HAVE . . . TO . . . UGHH . . .
AND IF THAT WASN'T ENOUGH, AT THAT VERY MOMENT, IN SUPER MAX'S SPARKLING BATHROOM . . .
!!!

HEH HEH HEH!

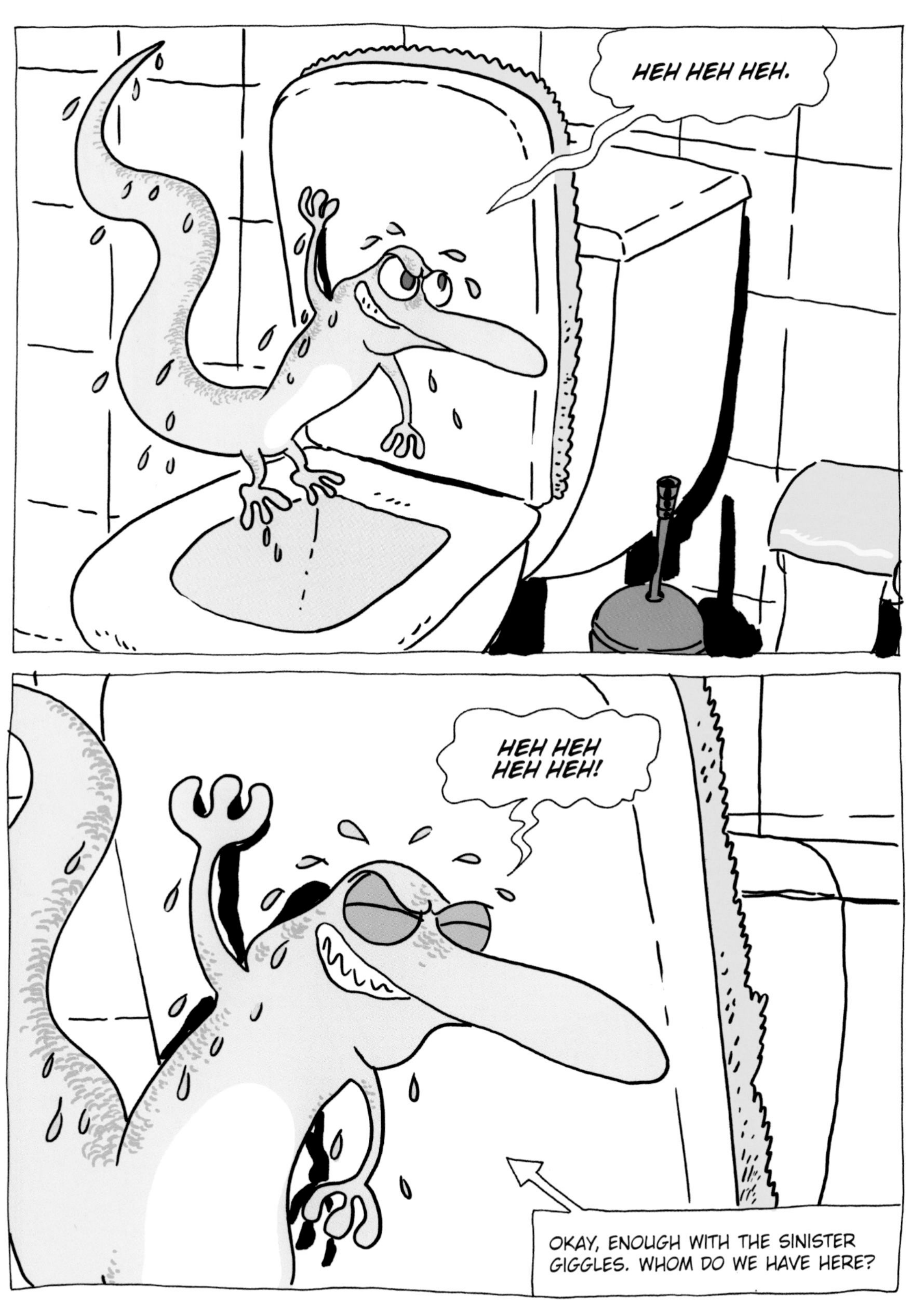
HEH HEH HEH.
HEH HEH HEH HEH!
OKAY, ENOUGH WITH THE SINISTER GIGGLES. WHOM DO WE HAVE HERE?

IT'S ARCHIBALD THE SCALY, MUTANT SEWER REPTILE AND SUPER MAX'S ARCHENEMY NUMBER NINETY-NINE!
THIS TIME, SUPER MAX WILL FEEL MY WRATH!
"ARCHENEMY NINETY-NINE"? BAH! I DESERVE TO BE IN THE TOP TEN! AND I WILL BE!
HEY, SUPER MAX! GUESS WHAT? I'VE GOT SOMETHING TO TELL YOU!

DO YOU HEAR ME, SUPER MAX?
THAT VOICE . . .
YUCK! AGAIN?
I'M HEEERE! WHAT ARE YOU WAITING FOR?
IT'S . . . IT'S . . .
ARCHIBALD THE SCALY!
HUH? DO WE KNOW EACH OTHER?

GET OUT OF MY PLACE! BACK TO THE SEWER!
YOUR PLACE?
OUCH!
BLAM
WHO DO YOU THINK YOU ARE?

WHERE DID YOU COME FROM? WHERE'S SUPER MAX?
WHA . . . ?
WHAT'S YOUR SCHEME, SEWER MUTANT?
AH! **SOMEONE** JUST MIGHT HAVE KIDNAPPED THE LOVELY OLIVIA OLSON AND HELD HER PRISONER . . .
1
IMAGINARY ARCHVILLAIN MEDAL
NOW WHAT GIVES? ***YOU'RE NOT SUPER MAX!***
YOU'RE . . .
A POTATO!?

WELL, UH, THAT MAY BE . . . BUT . . . WAIT! DID YOU SAY OLIVIA OLSON?
UPON HEARING THAT NAME, SUPER POTATO TRAVELS FARTHER INTO THE PAST. AND WITHOUT USING ANY TIME MACHINE!
OLIVIA OLSON!
SUPER POTATO REMEMBERS!!
AGAIN?
YEP.
CURSES– SUPER MAX!
ZOLTAN THE DARK! (ARCHENEMY NUMBER SIXTEEN.)
I GUESS YOU'VE COME TO SAVE ME?
THAT'S RIGHT! I DON'T GET WHY SUPERVILLAINS ARE SO SET ON CAPTURING YOU AGAIN AND AGAIN . . .

WELL, ZOLTAN, HOW DO YOU WANT TO DO THIS?
THE EASY WAY OR THE HARD WAY?
BAH! I'M OUTTA HERE. THAT GIRL'S NOT WORTH THE TROUBLE!
THEN YOU'RE TRULY A FOOL!
SUPER MAX HAS A TINY CRUSH ON THE LOVELY OLIVIA OLSON.
LISTEN—I DON'T LIKE YOUR STYLE, SUPER MAX.
YOU'RE BASICALLY A BIG BULLY. BUT . . . THANKS.
I'M ONLY DOING MY DUTY.

MAY I FLY YOU HOME?
IF I THINK YOU'RE ABOUT TO DROP ME, I'M GETTING ON A BUS.
NOT A CHANCE! I'M VERY STRONG. **SUPER** STRONG.

WHAT BEAUTIFUL MEMORIES! BUT LET'S RETURN TO THE SLIGHTLY MORE RECENT PAST . . .

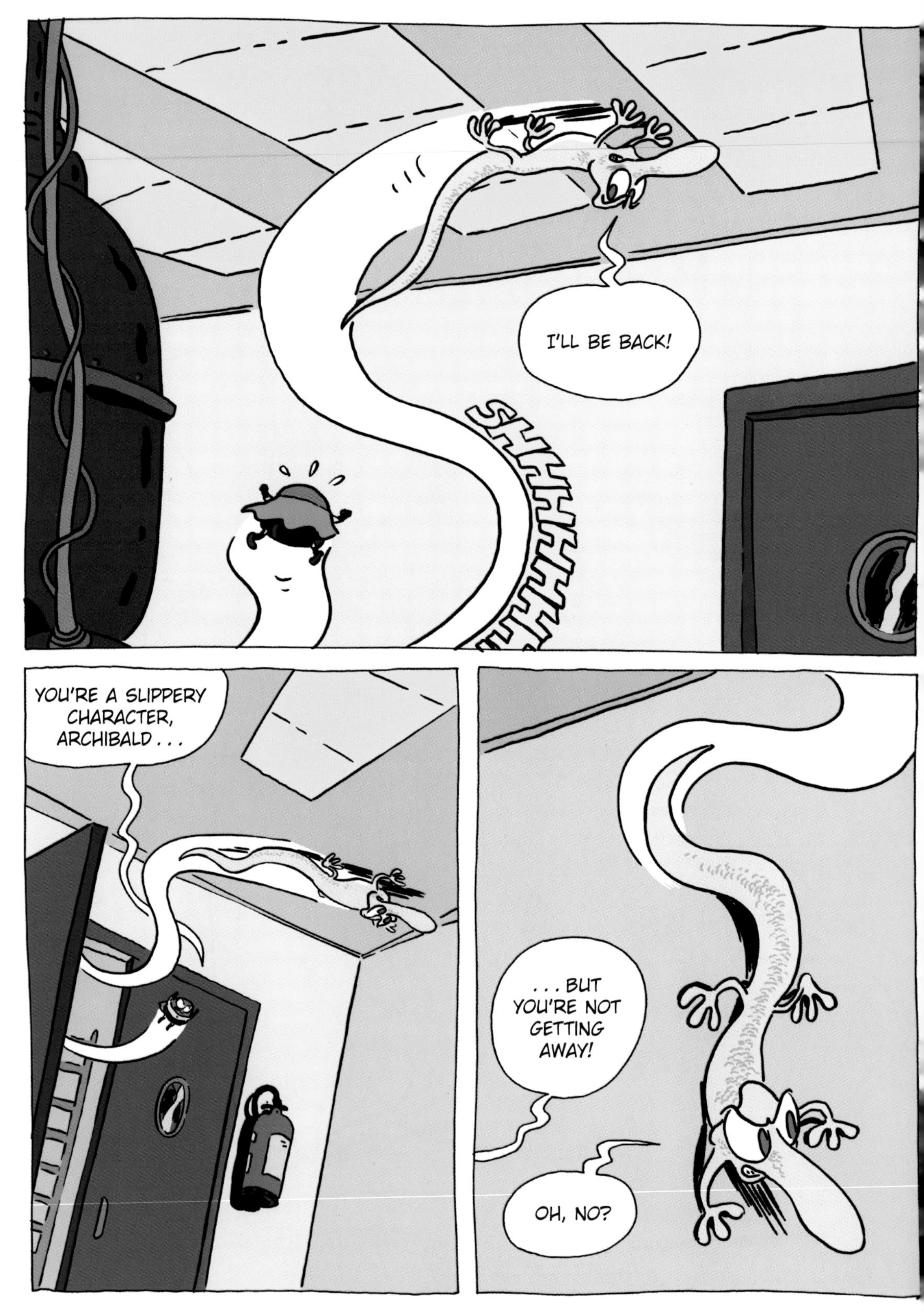
I'LL BE BACK!
SHHHHHHH
YOU'RE A SLIPPERY CHARACTER, ARCHIBALD . . .
. . . BUT YOU'RE NOT GETTING AWAY!
OH, NO?

YOU'LL NEVER TRAP ME!
PLOOF
HA! I'LL FOLLOW YOU . . .
. . . TO THE ENDS OF THE EARTH!
PLOOF

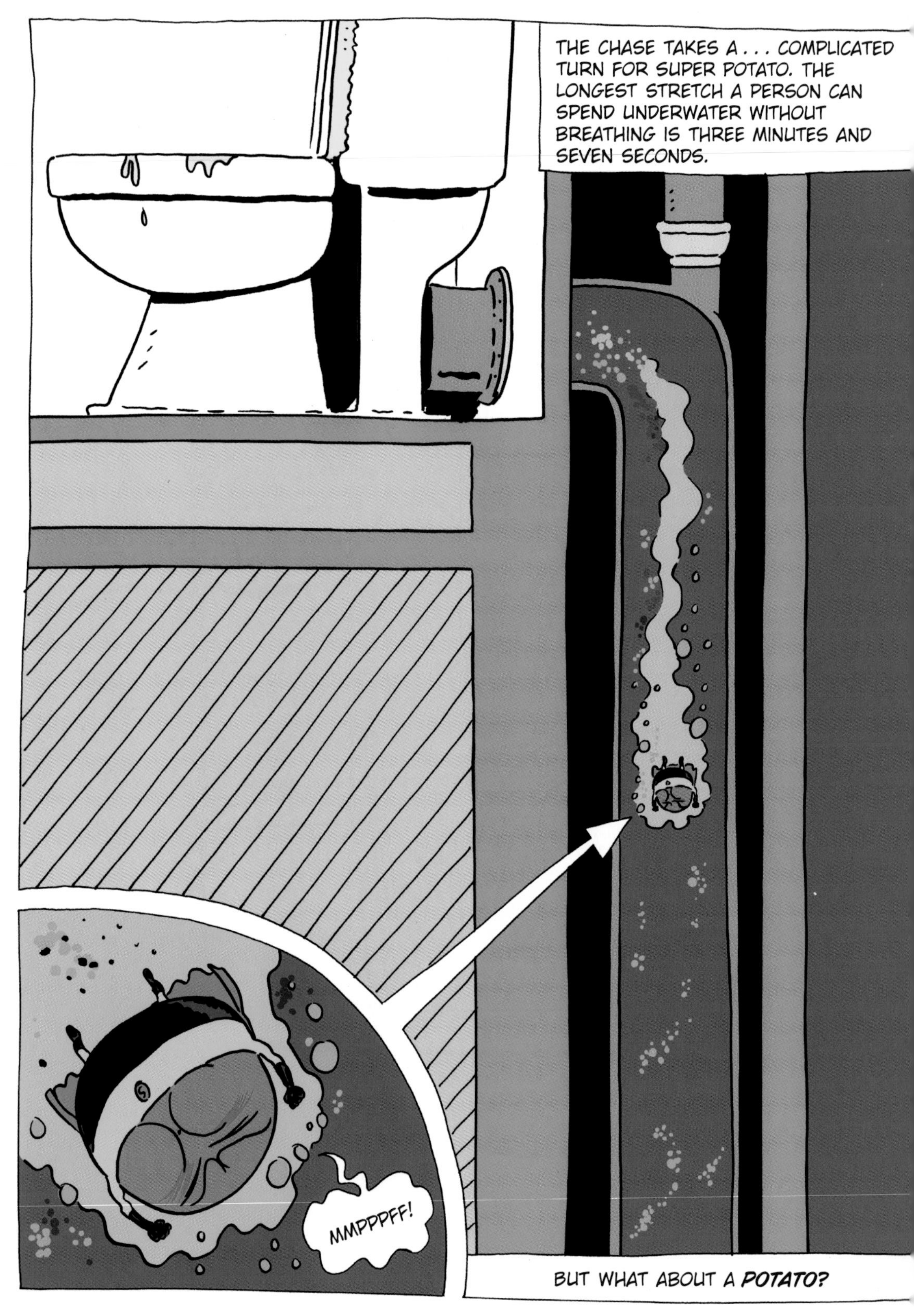
THE CHASE TAKES A . . . COMPLICATED TURN FOR SUPER POTATO. THE LONGEST STRETCH A PERSON CAN SPEND UNDERWATER WITHOUT BREATHING IS THREE MINUTES AND SEVEN SECONDS.
MMPPPFF!
BUT WHAT ABOUT A ***POTATO?***

FOR MORE THAN THIRTY SECONDS, SUPER POTATO DESCENDS THROUGH THE PIPE . . .

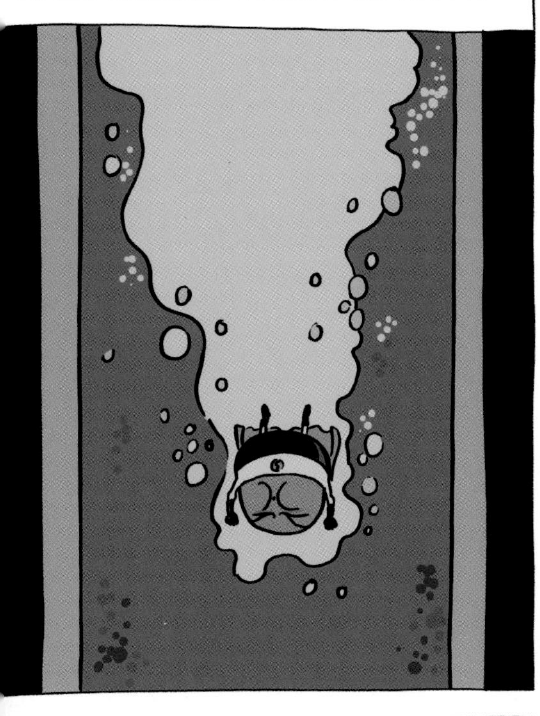

. . . UNTIL A STRONG CURRENT DRAGS HIM ALONG FOR ANOTHER FIFTY SECONDS.

AND SO, AFTER A FEW MINUTES . . .

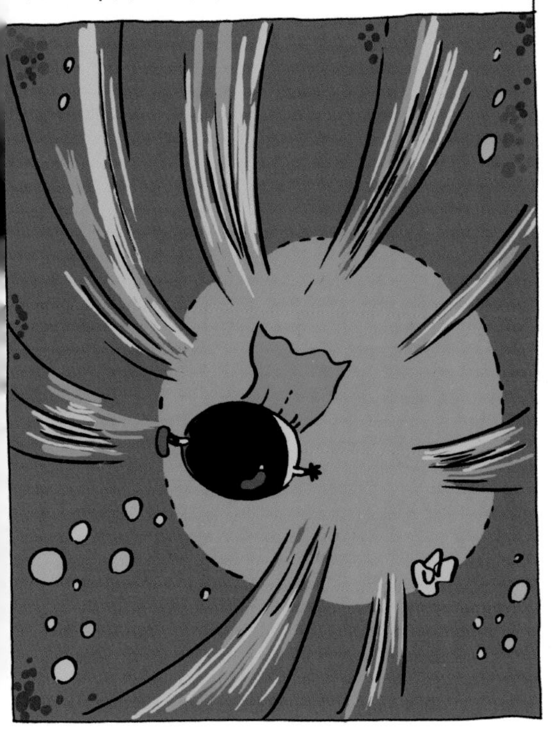

. . . HE'S ABLE TO STICK HIS HEAD ABOVE WATER AND TAKE A DEEP BREATH . . .

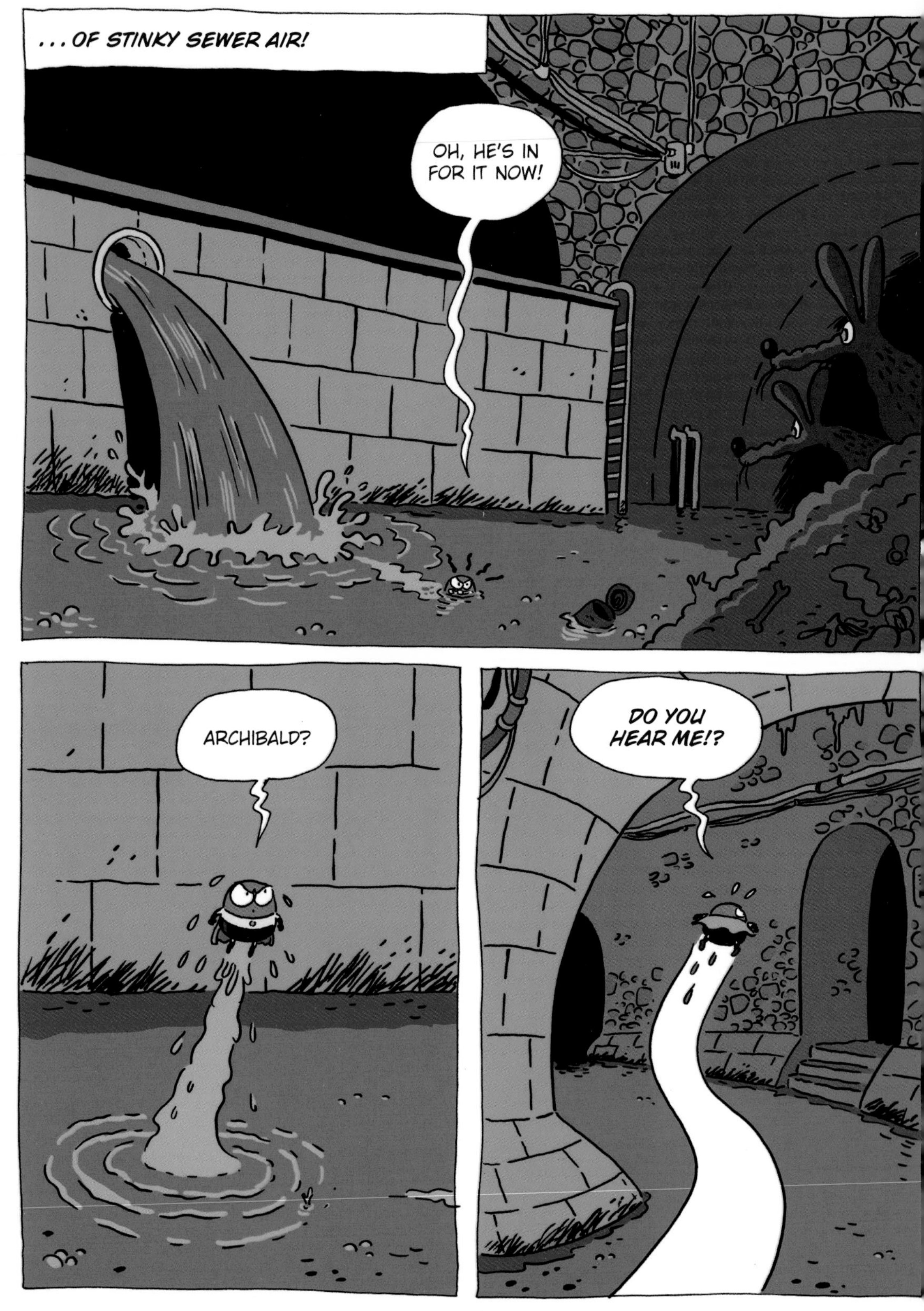
. . . OF STINKY SEWER AIR!
OH, HE'S IN FOR IT NOW!
ARCHIBALD?
DO YOU HEAR ME!?

ARCHIBALD!
WHAT HAPPENED TO SUPER MAX?
PLOP
BAH! TRY AND CATCH ME . . .
. . . IF YOU CAN.

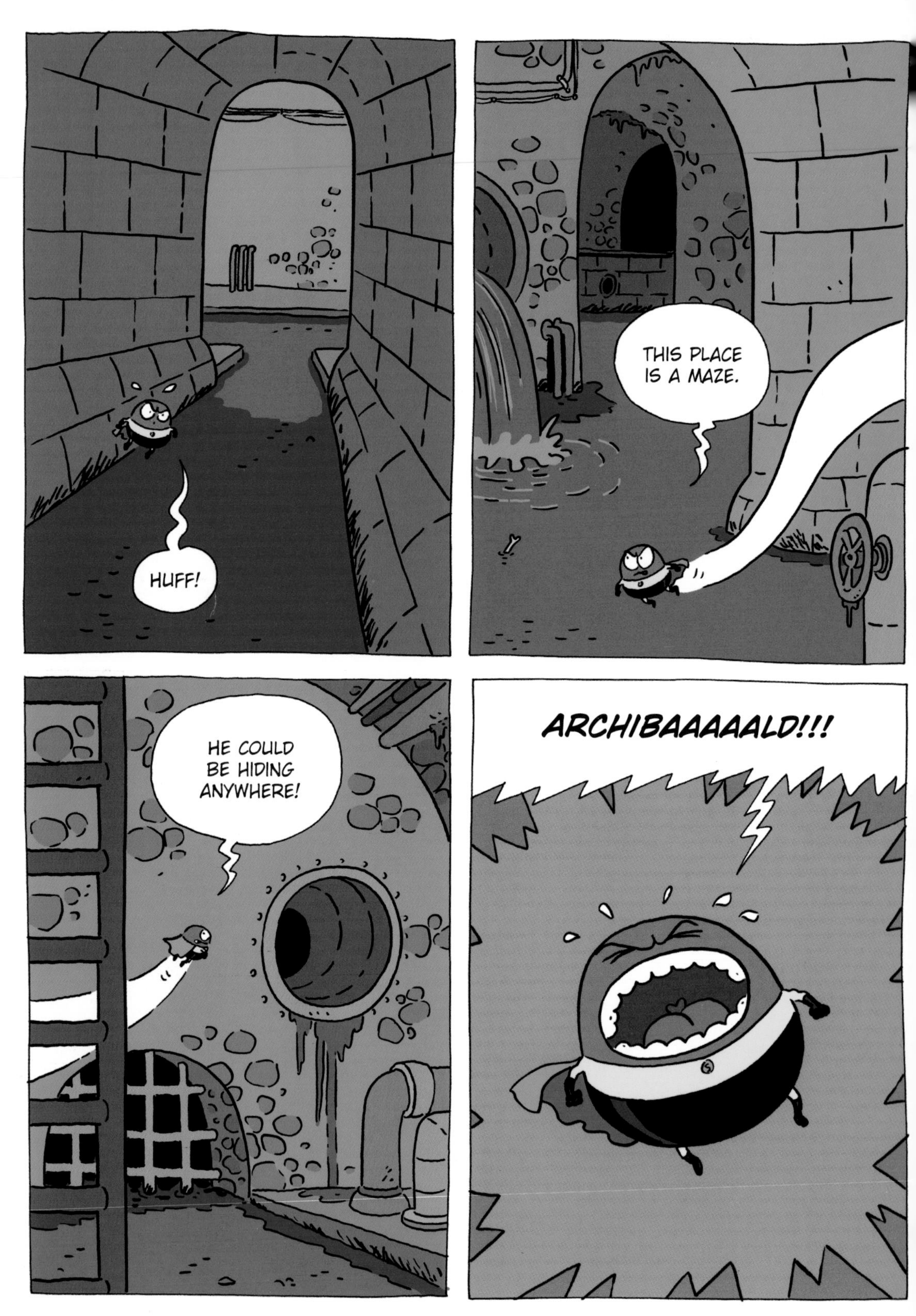
HUFF!
THIS PLACE IS A MAZE.
HE COULD BE HIDING ANYWHERE!
ARCHIBAAAAALD!!!

ARCHIBALD,
GET OUT HERE!
MEANWHILE, IN THE PRESENT DAY . . .
THERE'S NOT MUCH TIME LEFT . . .
YES, IT'S ALMOST LUNCH.
BUT LET'S GO BACK TO THE PAST, BECAUSE . . .
PSSSST. YOUUUNG ONNNNE.

ANOTHER TALKING REPTILE! IN THE SEWER, YOU CAN FIND ANYTHING.
AAAH!
I AM TORA TOOGA, NEON TORTOISE OF WIIIIISSSDOM, QUEEEEN OF TIIIME AND MEMMMORYYY.

THEEESE TUNNELS HOLLLD NOOOO SECRETS FOR MEEEE. I'VE BEEN HERE LONNNGER THAN ANNNYONNNNE CAN REEEMEMBERRRRR.
PERRRHAPSS I CAN HELLLLP YOOUUUU, BUUUUUT . . .
. . . OOOONLY AFFTER YOOUUU SOLLLLVE THREEEEE RIDDDDLESSSSSS.
THREE RIDDLES?
TO BE HONEST, I JUST WANT TO FIND ARCHIBALD THE SCALY. DO YOU KNOW HIM?

ARRRCHIIBALLLD? THAT MEANNN LIITTLE LIZZZZZZARD?
GO STRRRAIGHT. THENNN TAAAKE THE THIRRRRRD TUNNNEL ON THE RIIIGHT. ANND THENNN, THE FIIRRRRST TUNNNNEL ON YOUR LEFFFFT. TAAAKE THAAAT TO THE ENNNNNNNND.
BUT FIRST, THE RIIIDDLES.
RIDDDDLE NUMMMBERR ONNNE . . .
SORRY! SUPERHERO BUSINESS! GOTTA GO!
LATER! AND THANKS!

. . . YOU'RRRE WELLLLLLCOME . . . BYYYE . . .
LET'S SEE . . .
THE THIRD TUNNEL . . .
. . . ON THE RIGHT.

THEN THE NEXT LEFT . . .
AAH!
NO! NO! I DO NOT HAVE TIME FOR THIS!
GRRRRRRR!

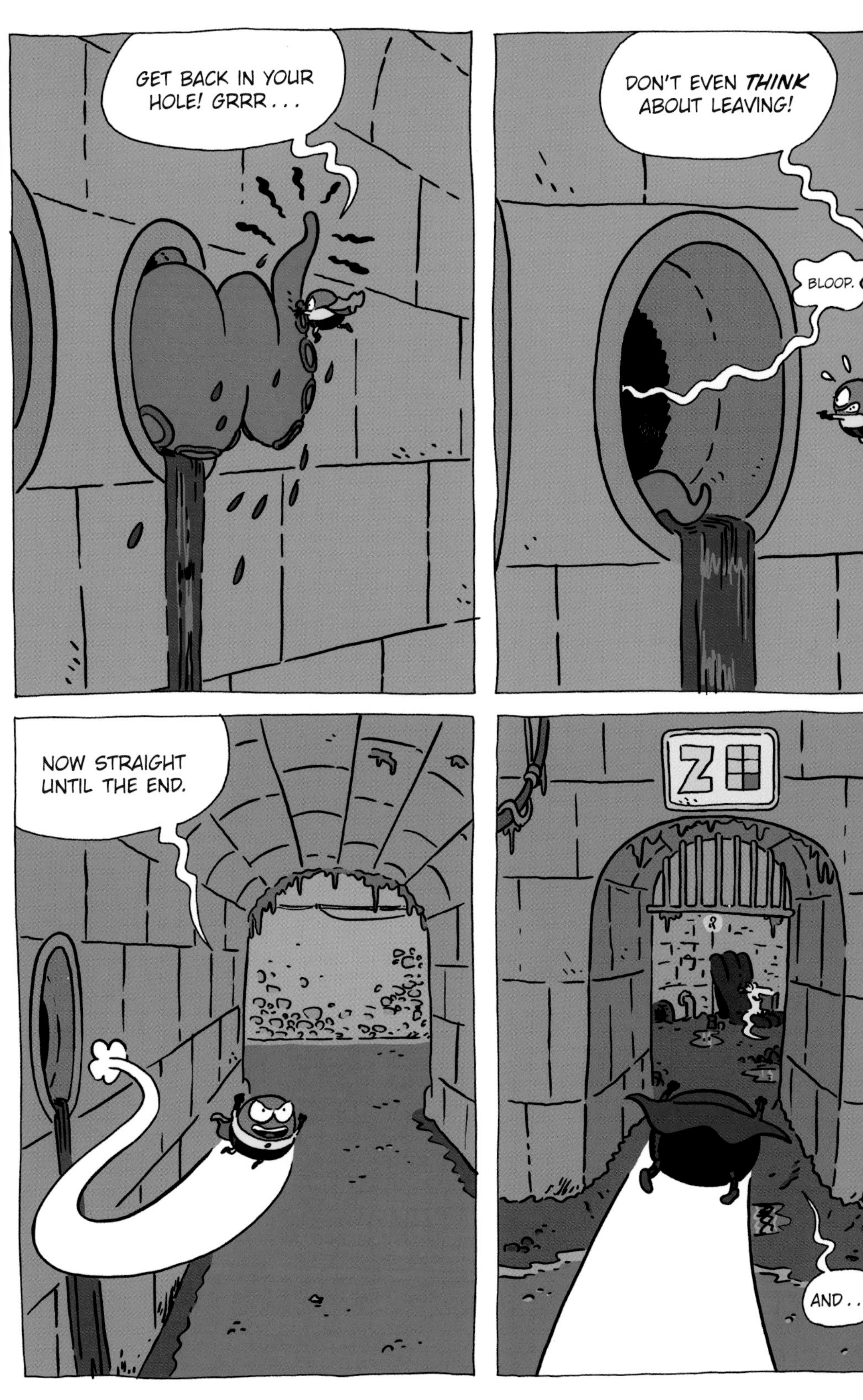
GET BACK IN YOUR HOLE! GRRR . . .
DON'T EVEN *THINK* ABOUT LEAVING!
BLOOP.
NOW STRAIGHT UNTIL THE END.
Z
AND . . .

CAUGHT YOU!
AAH!
HUH.
Home SWEET home
HOW TO BE EVIL BY COUNT CLAUS VON BADDIE, 98 PAGES, EVIL PRESS. CAN BE FOUND AT YOUR LOCAL LIBRARY.

YOU!!
LET HER GO, ARCHIBALD!
I'VE GOT TO ADMIT, I WAS NOT EXPECTING THIS. THAT THING IN THE CAPE SOUNDS ALMOST LIKE . . .
GET OUT OF HERE!
ZIP
PLOCK
WATCH IT! THAT'S NO WAY TO TREAT A GUEST.

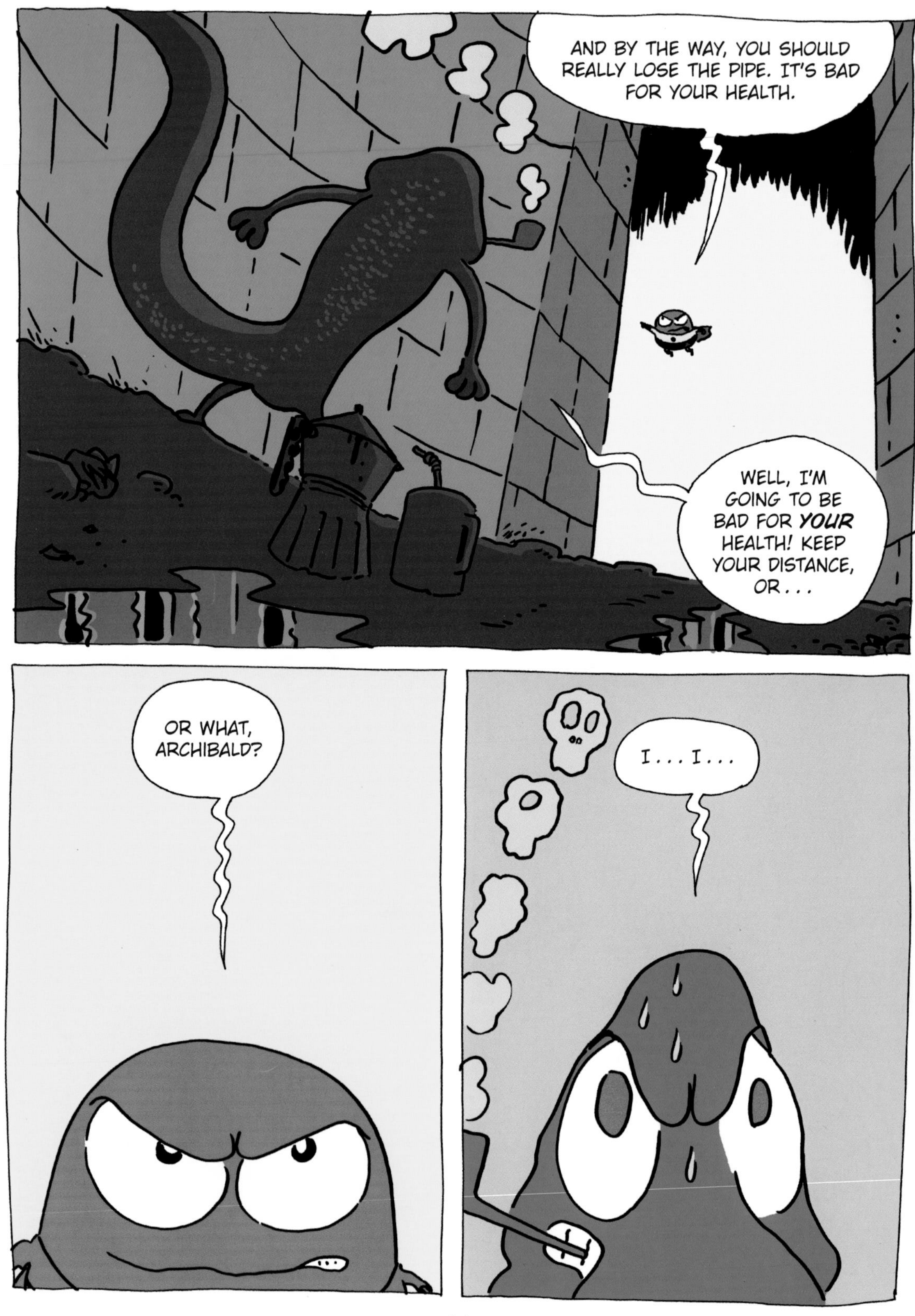
AND BY THE WAY, YOU SHOULD REALLY LOSE THE PIPE. IT'S BAD FOR YOUR HEALTH.
WELL, I'M GOING TO BE BAD FOR **YOUR** HEALTH! KEEP YOUR DISTANCE, OR . . .
OR WHAT, ARCHIBALD?
I . . . I . . .

I'LL EAT YOU BOTH! STARTING WITH THE GIRL!
HUH?
FEEDING TIME! AHHH HA HA HA HA HA!
EEEEE!
NOT HAPPENING, CREEP!
PLAM
OWWIE!

AAAH!
BOING
CROCK
UGH!
NICE FLYING KICK!
Home SWEET home
UHH . . . IT WAS AN ACCIDENT!
HE WAS GOING TO BITE ME!

DON'T WORRY. ARCHIBALD HAS A HARD HEAD. HE'LL GET OVER IT.
INDEED. ARCHIBALD THE SCALY WILL WAKE UP IN ABOUT THREE MINUTES, THOUGH HIS HEAD IS GOING TO BE A LITTLE FOGGY. HE WILL NOT REMEMBER KIDNAPPING OLIVIA OLSON NOR HIS CLASH WITH SUPER POTATO.
HE WILL CONTINUE TRYING TO BE AN ARCH SUPERVILLAIN, UNFORTUNATELY.
BUT BEFORE ALL THAT . . .
THANKS!
DON'T THANK ME YET. WE STILL HAVE TO GET OUT OF HERE.
AND THE QUICKEST WAY TO DO THAT IS . . .

UPWARD!

BLAM
HRRRRGHH!

AFTER YOU!
WELL, THANKS AGAIN.
I DON'T HAVE MUCH TIME BEFORE I HAVE TO RETURN HOME. BUT THERE'S A BUS STOP OVER THAT WAY.
YOU KNOW . . .

FROM THERE, EVERYTHING HAPPENS PRETTY FAST . . .

SUPER POTATO HEADS BACK TO HIS PLACE . . .

SUPER POTATO ARRIVES JUST IN TIME TO SEE THAT HIS TIME-TRAVEL MISSION TO AVOID BECOMING A POTATO HAS FAILED.
AAAH! I'M A POTATO!!!
GOODBYE, HAIR!
IT'S NOT SUCH A BIG DEAL.
AND HE ARRIVES JUST IN TIME TO NOT GET STUCK IN THE PAST.
AH! THERE IT IS.
ZRRRRT
TIME TO RETURN!

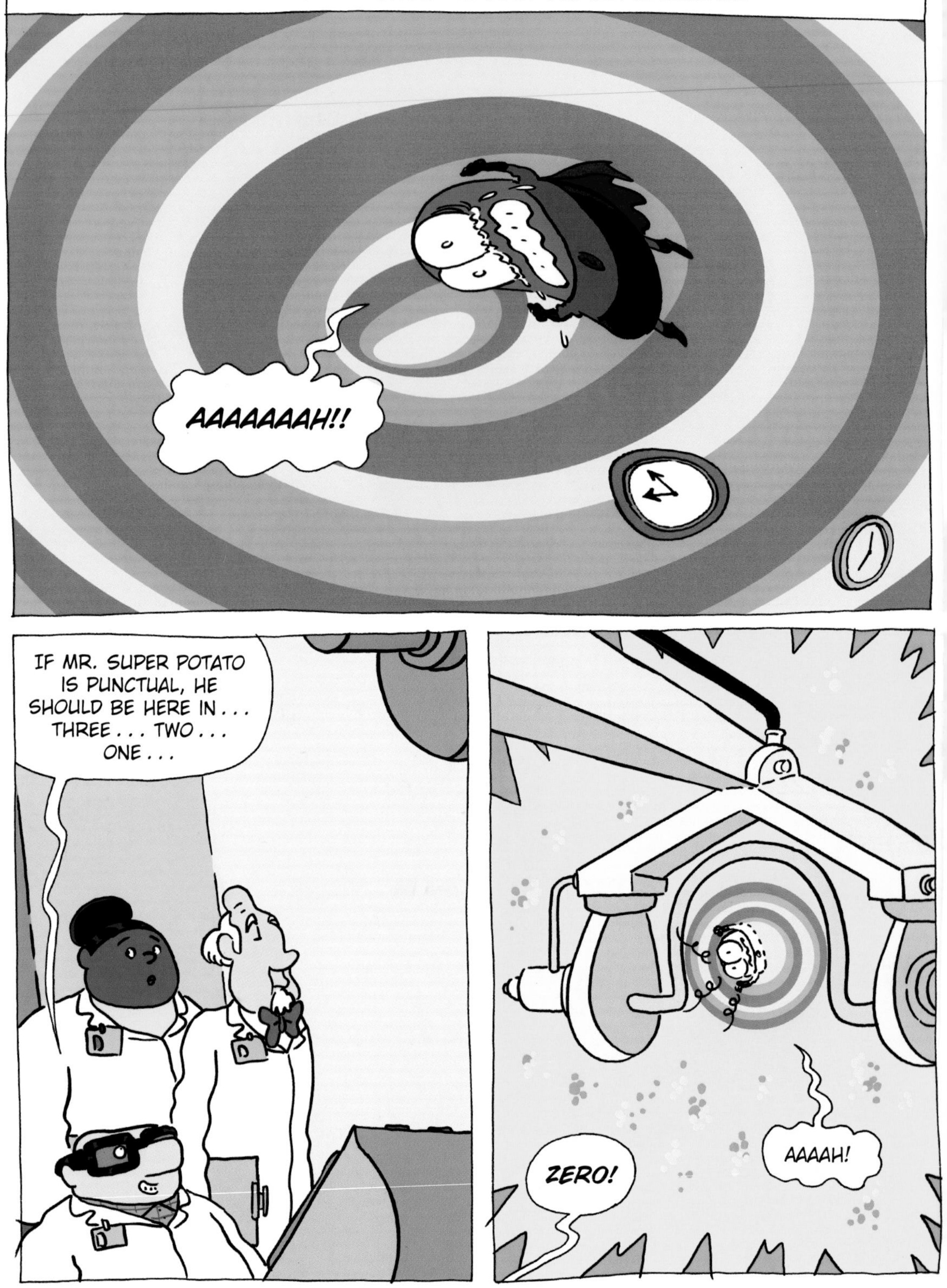
THE RETURN TRIP IS EXACTLY AS ROUGH AS THE FIRST ONE BUT IN REVERSE.
AAAAAAAH!!
IF MR. SUPER POTATO IS PUNCTUAL, HE SHOULD BE HERE IN . . . THREE . . . TWO . . . ONE . . .
ZERO!
AAAAH!

SUPER POTATO HAS ONLY DIPPED HIS TOES BACK INTO THE PRESENT WHEN . . .
PRRRRT
PRRRRT
PFFFFFF
AAAAAAH!
. . . THE SMALL-TIME MACHINE EXPLODES!*
BOOM
AAAH!
*THIS IS PROBABLY DUE TO A MANUFACTURING DEFECT.

UH . . . WHAT JUST HAPPENED?
BLUGGHHH!
WELL, IT SEEMS THAT SUPER POTATO'S JOURNEY INTO THE PAST HASN'T HAD A VERY BIG IMPACT. ALTHOUGH SOMEBODY IS SURE TO REMEMBER IT FOR A LONG, LONG TIME . . .
NOWWW-WHER WASSSS I??

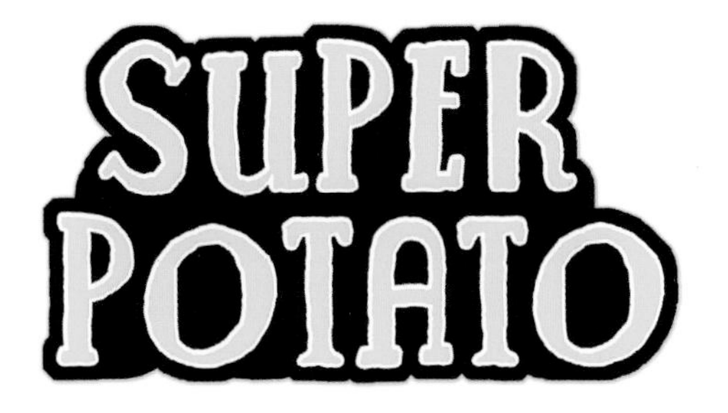

Also available:

THE EPIC ORIGIN OF SUPER POTATO

SUPER POTATO'S GALACTIC BREAKOUT

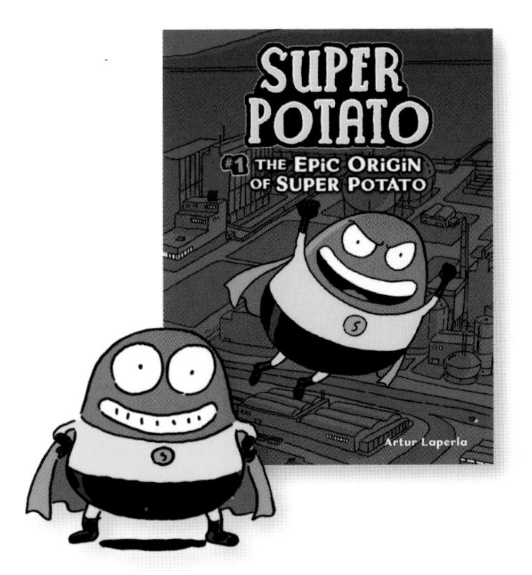

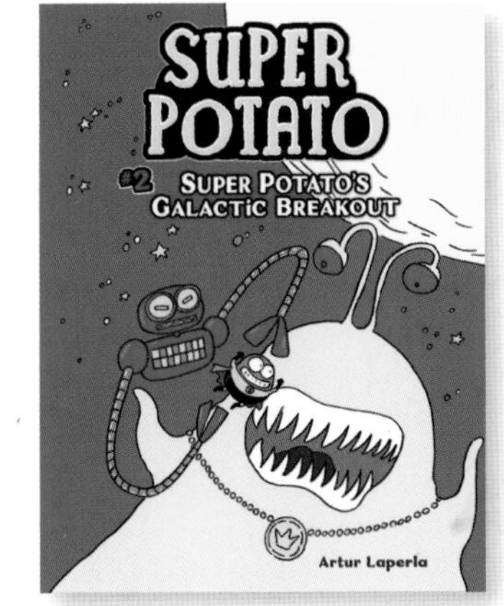